TWISTED

WHERE DID MY FAMILY GO?

Wil Mara

An imprint of Enslow Publishing

WEST **44** BOOKS™

CANCEL

THE VIDEOMANIAC   WHERE DID MY FAMILY GO?
HOUSE OF A MILLION ROOMS   THE GIRL WHO GREW NASTY THINGS
THE TIME TRAP

**Please visit our website, www.west44books.com.
For a free color catalog of all our high-quality books,
call toll free 1-800-542-2595 or fax 1-877-542-2596.**

Cataloging-in-Publication Data

Names: Mara, Wil.
Title: Where did my family go? / Wil Mara.
Description: New York : West 44, 2020. | Series: Twisted
Identifiers: ISBN 9781538383650 (pbk.) | ISBN 9781538383605 (library bound) |
  ISBN 9781538383551 (ebook)
Subjects: LCSH: Sick--Juvenile fiction. | Families--Juvenile fiction. |
  Supernatural--Juvenile fiction.
Classification: LCC PZ7.M373 Wh 2020 | DDC [F]--dc23

Published in 2020 by
Enslow Publishing LLC
101 West 23rd Street, Suite #240
New York, NY 10011

Copyright © 2020 Enslow Publishing LLC

Editor: Caitie McAneney
Designer: Rachel Rising
Interior Layout: Seth Hughes

Photo Credits: Cover (background) Borislav Bajkic/Shutterstock.com; Cover (family)
Ysbrand Cosijn/Shutterstock.com; Back Cover (background) STILLFX/Shutterstock.com;
p.5 (family icon) nelelena/Shutterstock.com.

Printed in the United States of America

CPSIA compliance information: Batch #CS18W44: For further information contact
Enslow Publishing LLC, New York, New York at 1-800-542-2595.

TWISTED

For Lisa Krauze—thanks for all the help.

Michael Cooper was sick. Like, *really* sick.

He lay in his bed all hot and sweaty. It was about the grossest feeling in the world. His pajamas stuck to his body. And it felt like there was a layer of slime on his skin. If he had to get up, the sheets felt like they were being peeled off of him. And he *reeked*. He couldn't stand anyone who reeked—and now *he* reeked. But he couldn't do much about it. If he took a shower, he'd just start sweating again afterward. So what was the point?

There was nothing he hated more than being sick. He had a very busy life. Far too busy to be lying in bed all day. He went to school like any other kid. He didn't love school, but he didn't hate it, either. He liked his teachers (most of them). And he liked his classes (most of them). He liked seeing his friends. He liked gym and recess. And his grades were pretty good (most of them).

When he wasn't in school, he did all sorts of fun stuff. He played baseball a lot. Football and basketball, too. He rode his bike or his skateboard. He went swimming every summer, usually in someone's pool. There was also a big lake on the other side of town. It had a rope hanging from a tree and everything. You could swing on it and then drop into the water. That was fantastic. And in the winter, there was sleigh riding and fort building and snowball fighting.

There were a lot of fun things to do at home, too. He had both an Xbox and a PlayStation. There was a huge TV in the living room. And he had a pretty big one in his room, too. He also had a laptop, an iPad, and an iPhone. His dad even had some cool stuff in the basement. There was a pool table, some vintage video games, and two vintage pinball machines. His dad was always asking him to come and play with him. Michael pretended like he wasn't interested. But he really was. He just couldn't *tell* his dad he was interested. It was, like, one of the most important rules of being a kid. You just couldn't.

With all this stuff in his life, how could he lay in bed all day? Getting sick just wasn't fair. His head ached so much he thought it might crack open. His stomach felt like it had an ocean rolling around inside. And he had no idea his nose could make so much snot. He would've given anything to feel better. *Anything.*

But there was no magical cure. He'd been told this over and over. His dad said it, his mom said it, even his sister said it. Time—that's what it took. Time and rest and medicine. Michael knew this, but he was still unhappy about it. And because he was unhappy, he was making everybody else unhappy.

It wasn't like this was the first time he'd ever been sick. He had a bad throat infection when he was five. And chicken pox when he was ten. But back then, he liked everyone taking care of him. It was nice to be fussed over. It made him feel like a prince or something. But now he just found everything annoying.

Which was really too bad. If he hadn't been so busy acting like a grouch, he might have noticed some of the strange things that had started happening. Like with his Converse sneakers, which were lying on the floor. When he took them off two days ago, they were white.

Now they were blue.

"Mom!" Michael yelled from his bed. "*MOM*!!!"

She opened the door a moment later. "Yes, my darling child?" she said, sounding tired. He knew she was being sarcastic.

"I want soup!"

His mom was wearing a plain T-shirt, faded jeans, and flip-flops. Her flame-orange hair was fairly short all around. But she also used gel to make a little point near the front. Michael called this "Mom's horn."

"And how do nice kids ask their mothers for soup?" she asked.

"Chicken noodle," Michael replied, wiping his nose with a tissue. Then he tossed it into the garbage can next to the bed. The can was already overloaded with about a million others. "And not so hot this time. That last bowl was way too hot."

His mom put on a smile, but there was nothing cheerful about it.

"Whatever you wish, Prince Michael," she said. Then she sighed. "Anything else?"

"Yeah, tell Corinne to come in here."

"Since you're asking so nicely, sure…"

She rolled her eyes and went out. A few minutes later, Michael's sister came in. She was skinny like their mom. Her eyes were a beautiful green, and her brown hair was long and straight. She also had a little cluster of freckles on either side of her nose.

She put her hands on her hips.

"What do you want now?"

After she said this, she pressed her lips together hard. This turned them into a short, straight line.

"My tablet," he said. "You have it in your room."

"I'm using it to do summer school homework right now!"

"I want to watch a movie online."

Corinne pointed to the TV. "Watch a movie on *that*!"

"I don't want to watch on that. I want to watch on my tablet, with my earbuds."

"Michael, come on…"

"Use your laptop for your homework."

"It's at school!" Corinne said. "I forgot it!"

"Then I guess you're outta luck," Michael told her. He took a sip of water from a *Star Wars* cup that was on his nightstand.

"You're such a brat!" she shot back. "Ever since you've been sick, you've been *impossible*!"

She turned and stomped out before Michael could say anything further. When she returned, she just about threw the tablet at him. Then she stormed out again, mumbling something under her breath.

His dad came in about ten minutes after that. Neil Cooper was tall like his son. They both also had very dark hair. His, however, was starting to show some silver streaks these days.

"Hey, sport."

Michael was holding the buds next to his ears. "I'm just about to watch a movie," he said. "Can you come back later?"

His dad crossed his arms and smiled. Then he leaned against the doorway.

"I understand you're being quite the grump."

"I feel terrible."

"I'm sure you do. I've been sick before, so I know how you feel."

Michael shook his head. "No you don't.

Not like this. I feel like I'm gonna die."

"You're not going to die, Mike."

"I *feel* like I am."

"Yeah, well, you're not. You'll get better, and everything will be fine. You'll see."

Then his dad came into the room and started cleaning up. He was the kind of person who couldn't help doing stuff like this. If a picture was hanging just a little crooked, he'd straighten it. If someone left a cup or a bowl in the sink, he'd put it in the dishwasher.

He gathered up Michael's dirty clothes, opened the closet door, and threw them in the hamper. Then he took out the garbage can with all the tissues. When he came back, it was empty. Finally, he picked up the Converse sneakers and headed for the closet again.

"Hey, wait a second," Michael said.

"Huh?"

"Those sneakers…" He pointed at them. "They're not mine."

"What are you talking about?"

"Mine are *white*."

His dad held them up. They were a dark navy with white soles.

"Michael, they're blue."

"I know they're blue. But mine are *white*, so they're not mine!"

"Mike, you own a half dozen different pairs of Converse." His dad opened the closet door again. Then he pointed toward the closet floor. "See?"

"Yeah, but I don't have any that are *blue*. And I remember taking off the white ones last night."

His dad shrugged. "I don't know what to tell you, sport. These are your size. And I saw you wearing them yesterday, not the white ones."

Michael was about to argue the point further. Then he paused.

"Wait…no. I remember picking out…hang on. Are you sure?"

"Yes, Mike, I'm sure." He gave Michael a look. Then he added, "And I know these are yours because your mom and I got them for your birthday."

"You did?"

"We did."

His dad tossed them into the closet with the others and closed the door again.

"Anyway, I just came in to, um…well, to tell you you're being a real pain in the butt to everybody."

"I…feel…*awful*," Michael reminded him.

"And we're all trying to help you get better. Just remember that, okay?"

Michael put in his earbuds. "I'm watching

my movie now."

His dad looked like he was going to say something more. Instead, he just shook his head and went out.

Michael got up in the middle of the night to go to the bathroom. This was around three o'clock.

He turned himself in the bed and threw his legs over. His toes touched the carpet, and that was good. He loved the feel of carpet under his bare feet. His mom always kept the carpet in their house nicely vacuumed. That was also good. He had a friend, Baker, who lived in a house that was beyond disgusting. It didn't look like anyone *ever* vacuumed his carpet. Michael couldn't imagine letting his bare feet anywhere near it.

He shuffled out of the room and turned

left. His head was still aching like crazy. And his nose still felt about ten pounds heavier than usual. But at least his stomach had stopped churning and turning.

The hallway was quiet and dark except for a small night-light. Michael's eyes were half closed because he was still half asleep. He always thought the same thing during these middle-of-the-night pit stops. *I gotta get back to bed as soon as possible*. He needed sleep. He loved sleep.

About halfway down the hall, he turned left again.

BAM!!!

He bounced away and went down with his arms flying.

"What the *heck*?!"

His eyes sprung open all the way now. He still wasn't completely awake. But he was getting there fast.

He looked up and saw nothing but a solid wall. It had tan-and-blue wallpaper with lots of flowers. His mom picked it out. His dad hated it. Michael could tell at the time, but his dad never said so. There were also two framed pictures of his Aunt Jennie. In one, she was at the top of a mountain she'd just hiked. There was a huge smile on her face. In the other, she was canoeing down a white-water river. Same smile, like she'd just scored a goal at the World Cup or something.

But none of that's supposed to be there, Michael thought. He felt more confused than he ever had in his life. *It's supposed to be on the OTHER side of the hall! And the bathroom door is supposed to be on—*

He turned and saw that the door was right next to him.

"Wait…what?!" He jumped to his feet. "How is this *HERE*?!" he whispered sharply.

He reached out and touched the door. He did this gently, as if it might explode. Then he pushed it a little. It drifted back an inch or two, its hinges groaning.

He looked to the pictures of Aunt Jennie again. Then to the door. Then the pictures. Then the door.

No, this isn't right…this isn't right at ALL.

Michael pushed the door back all the way and stepped inside. There was another night-light in here. It was a plain one, although it used to be a Mickey Mouse light. His mom changed it one day. She said he was getting too old for a Mickey Mouse light. Michael went along with this and didn't say anything. But he would've been okay if Mickey had stayed. Mickey was *classic*.

He looked all around the bathroom. Everything seemed to be where it should—shower, toilet, towel rack, toothbrushes. He opened the cabinet under the sink. Everything in there seemed right, too. A hair dryer was lying with its cord wrapped around it. Extra rolls of toilet paper were stacked in one corner. Next to that was his dad's shaving kit in a worn leather bag.

He looked at himself in the mirror. His dark hair was as tough as the bristles on a brush. And it usually stood straight up. But it spiked ridiculously in every direction now. And he could see how tired he still was. His eyes were red and puffy. They stung a little bit, too.

Have to go back to bed…have to go back to bed…
He decided that he'd been wrong about

the door. It *was* supposed to be on the right side of the hall. A part of him still didn't believe this. But he was in no mood to argue with himself at the moment. So he did what he came to do. Then he flushed and washed his hands.

He shuffled back to his room and fell into bed. As he spun down into darkness, a voice spoke out in his mind.

The door is not supposed to be on that side. And you know it. It's NOT…

He ignored this. Just a wacky part of his brain trying to scare him. It was funny, really—the idea that a door could change places.

Crazy, he told himself.

Then he was snoring away.

Michael woke up a little after eight o'clock the next morning. He felt about the same. It was a Saturday, which was nice enough. But then he remembered it was the middle of summer vacation. And he was sick. Who cared what day it was?

He set his bare feet on the carpet again. He scratched his head and rubbed his eyes. Then started down the hall for another trip to the bathroom. He started to turn left, but stopped himself.

No, that's not it, he thought. He opened his eyes fully and saw the two pictures of Aunt Jennie. There she was, smiling as big as ever.

He turned the other way, and there was the bathroom door. It still didn't seem quite right to him. But then in another way it *did*.

Whatever, he told himself. *It's summertime. I don't need to really use my brain again until September.*

He went in and did his business. This time he washed his face and brushed his teeth, too. It all took less than two minutes. Then he went down the hall and into the kitchen.

His dad was at the stove, cooking omelets. There was also bacon frying in a skillet. Everything smelled fantastic. His dad loved to cook, but he never had time during the week. So he cooked on the weekends.

"Hey, junior," he said to Michael with a smile. He was wearing an apron that had oil splattered on it. Printed on the front was:

I'D TELL YOU THE RECIPE, BUT THEN I'D HAVE TO KILL YOU.

He had a lot of recipes that he'd created himself. He was very proud of them, too. Michael liked most of the stuff his dad made.

"Hey," Michael replied. He got into his usual seat at the round table.

"How are you feeling now?"

Michael did a seesaw motion with his hand. So-so. "Can you make me an omelet, too?"

"I sure can."

Michael's mom came in at that moment.

"Is mine ready, hon?" she asked her husband.

"Just about."

"Good, I'm starving. Thank you." Then she turned to Michael. "And how are you this morning?"

Michael was texting his best friend Zack as he waited for his food. "The same," he said without looking up from the screen.

"Did you sleep well?"

"Yeah." He finished the text and waited a few seconds. Zack didn't answer right away. That meant he was still asleep.

Michael put the phone down (face up, of course). Then he smiled and said, "But the weirdest thing happened to me during the night."

There was a bowl of assorted fruit in the center of the table. There were apples, oranges, bananas, and grapes.

His mom helped herself to a banana and started peeling it. "Oh yeah?" she asked. "What was that?"

"I thought the bathroom door was on the other side of the hall." He grabbed an apple and took a bite.

His dad froze. It looked like he'd been hit by an alien stun ray. Then he turned around, his face wrinkled by disbelief.

"You *what*?"

Michael looked back at him and laughed. Then he looked at his mom.

"Yeah," he said, nodding. "I walked right into the wall!"

"That's crazy," his mom told him.

"I know. And I was sure it was supposed to be on the other side." He took another bite of the apple. "I *still* feel that way a little bit."

Michael's dad set down an omelet in front of his wife.

"It might be because you've been sick," he said. "Or it could be something else entirely. Hmm…you didn't get clunked with a baseball, did you? Maybe during your game the other day?"

He started feeling around Michael's head. Then Michael swatted his hand away.

"No, I didn't get *clunked* with a baseball."

"Just checking."

His dad returned to the stove. He broke two fresh eggs into the pan. They sizzled and popped as he tossed the shells into the garbage.

"Well, I'm sure the bathroom door is where it's supposed to be," his mom said.

"Yeah, I'm sure it is, too," Michael replied. But he felt weird as he said this. It was like the feeling he got when he told a lie. He didn't lie much. He just wasn't that kind of a kid. But when he did, his stomach sort of ached. He felt bad, but he also felt *wrong*. Like a lie was some kind of poison that affected everything. He knew the bathroom door was in the right place. And yet there was this other part of him. A part that really thought it *wasn't*.

A few minutes later his dad put his omelet in front of him. The noise made him snap out of his thoughts.

"Here you are," his dad said. "Enjoy."

"Thanks."

Michael grabbed his fork and went to dig in. But just before the fork hit the food, he stopped.

"Wait a minute…"

Both his parents turned. "What's wrong?" his mom asked.

"This is cheese."

His dad nodded. "Yeah, so?"

"I hate cheese."

The look of confusion returned to his dad's face. "Huh?"

"No you don't," his mom told him.

"Yes I do! I can't stand cheese!"

"Michael," his mom said very calmly. "You *love* cheese."

"You have cheese omelets two or three times a week," his dad added.

"No I don—" Michael began. Then he stopped and thought it over. "Do I? Wait…no. No I don't! I *don't…like…CHEESE*!"

His mom held one of his hands in hers. "Michael, listen to me. You *do* like cheese! Believe me, I'm your mother!"

"Mike, she's right," his dad said. "I don't know what you're thinking at the moment. You're confused or something. But I swear to you, you like cheese. You have it all the time."

Michael looked at his food again.

"I do?"

His dad nodded. "You sure do."

"Umm…okay."

He studied the omelet for a few seconds. He looked like a scientist checking out a new species of bug or something. Then he poked it with his fork. He turned the fork and cut off a small piece. It was steaming hot. He brought it up to his nose and sniffed. *Nothing*, he thought. *It smells like absolutely nothing.*

He tried to remember what cheese smelled like. Was it really true that he didn't hate it? That he ate it all the time? If so, then how come he couldn't remember anything about it?

"Try it!" his mom said, smiling. "You'll see. Meanwhile, I'll go let the dog in."

"All right." He put the piece of omelet into his mouth. He chewed it around a few times. *It still tastes like nothing*, he thought. He waited for that great burst of flavor you get when you first bite something. But it never came.

"Isn't it good?" his dad asked.

Michael nodded. "Sure, it's great," he said. He didn't want to hurt his dad's feelings.

"Good," his dad replied. Then he went to the sink to wash the pan.

His mom returned a moment later.

"Okay, our pup is in," she said.

Michael looked but didn't see her. He turned in his chair and patted his thighs.

"Come on, Ranger! In here!"

His parents both stopped what they were doing again.

"Ranger?" his dad said. "Who's Ranger?"

Michael laughed. "Whaddaya mean, 'Who's Ranger'? Ranger's our d—"

The dog came into the kitchen and trotted to Michael's side of the table. It was a medium-sized hound, light brown with white paws. It also had the friendliest, happiest face a dog could possibly have.

The moment Michael saw it, his eyes grew as big as ping-pong balls. "Whose dog is *this*?"

The dog stopped and plunked its butt into a sitting position. It seemed confused by his reaction.

"What are you talking about?" his mom asked. "This is Daisy!"

"Daisy?!" he repeated. "*WHO'S DAISY*?"

Now his mom looked really worried. "Michael," she said softly, stroking the fur behind the dog's head. "This is *our dog*. Y'know—*Daisy*? We've had her for the last seven years?"

Michael stared at Daisy with fear and confusion swimming in his eyes.

"No…" he said quietly. "No, this isn't Range—I mean, this isn't our dog. Ranger has black fur. And she's smaller!"

"Michael," his dad replied, "this is our dog."

"No," Michael insisted, shaking his head. Then he began rising from his seat. "Something's going on here. Something really weird. The dog…the omelet…the bathroom door…"

His dad came over and put an arm around his shoulders.

"Okay, don't freak out," he said. "You're probably just tired out from being sick. Did you get enough sleep last night?"

He thought about it for a second, but nothing came. He usually had an excellent memory, so this was also very weird.

"I…I don't know…I remember walking into the wall and all that. But…why can't I remember anything else?"

"Did you have a bad dream?" his mom asked.

"I don't know. No, I don't think…umm…" He shook his head in frustration. "Arrgh! I just can't remember!"

"It's okay, son," his dad said. Then he turned Michael around and led him out of the kitchen. "Maybe you should just go back to bed for a bit. Sleep a little more."

Michael felt like he was in a daze. One question kept repeating itself in his mind—

What is happening to me?

"Okay, yeah," he said as they crossed into his bedroom. "Maybe that's…a good…idea…"

He dropped onto the mattress, felt the

pillow come up to his face.

Then darkness filled in around him, and he was out.

Michael woke up again a few hours later. It was nearly one o'clock in the afternoon.

He'd had the weirdest dream. He'd eaten so many hot dogs that he turned into one (just like his mom always said he would). Then Ranger (or *Daisy, or…well, whatever,* he thought) sniffed him out and started chasing him. Michael ran around the house crying tears of yellow mustard. But he wasn't fast enough. He woke up just before she took a big bite out of him.

Michael shivered as he walked out of his room. He padded down the hallway and turned right to go into the bathroom.

BAM!!!

He bounced off the wall and fell in a heap onto the floor.

"What the *heck*?!"

The door had moved again. It was back on the other side.

He got to his feet quickly. "What…is…going…*on*…here?" he said. There was a wobble in his voice.

Other things had changed, too. The pictures of Aunt Jennie, for example. There were three now instead of two. And she wasn't hiking or rafting in any of them. One was a baby picture. The second was of her graduating college. And the third was from her wedding. Michael didn't recognize the man she married, though. He was tall and kind of goofy-looking. Michael never saw him before in his life.

"This can't be happening," he said to himself, backing away slowly. "It *can't* be…"

He went into the bathroom. Seconds later he came running back out.

"I PEED IN THE SINK!" he cried. "I PEED IN THE SINK!"

He zoomed down the hall and into the kitchen again. Finding no one in there, he continued to the living room. His dad was just getting up from his easy chair when he came in.

"Michael, what are you yelling abou—"

"I peed in the sink!" Michael said, pointing in that direction.

"You *WHAT*?"

"I didn't realize because I didn't turn on the light!"

"Michael—"

"It was just like with the door! The toilet and the sink *switched places*!"

His dad brushed past him and started toward the hall. "I'd better clean that up before your mother finds out." Then he stopped to think. "Bleach…I need some bleach from the baseme—"

"*Dad, didn't you hear me*?!" Michael bawled. "The sink and the toilet aren't in the same place anym—"

"What's all the noise about?" someone asked from the stairs. Michael recognized his sister Corinne's voice right away. But when he turned, he found someone else standing there.

He stumbled back, hit the corner of the coffee table, and went down. Then he got to his feet again.

"*Who…WHO ARE YOU*?" he demanded, pointing a shaking finger.

The Corinne he knew had long brown hair and green eyes. This person had short blond hair and blue eyes. She was also wearing flip-flops, which the real Corinne hated. And this girl had absolutely no makeup on. The real Corinne would never let anyone see her without makeup.

She made a face. "Seriously, Michael?"

"D-dad, who is this?"

His dad stared. "Michael, it's your sister."

"No it's not! *No it's not!*"

Corinne shook her head and started down the stairs again. As she did, Michael backed further away from her.

"You shouldn't be here!" he said, still pointing. "Whoever you are!"

"Michael, *stop*," she told him.

But he wasn't listening. He backed up all the way to the wall. Then he slid against it until he reached the doorway to the kitchen. He took one more look at the girl. The terror in his eyes was as bright as the surface of the sun.

He turned and ran back into his room.

Michael slammed his door shut and locked it. Breathing hard, he sat down on the edge of the bed.

I'm not going crazy, he chanted in his mind. *I'm not going crazy.*

He buried his face in his hands for a few minutes. Then he took them down and looked carefully around the room.

Has anything ELSE changed? he wondered. It was a horrifying thought.

There was a picture of him and Zack on the wall. They had been best friends forever—literally. Their parents were all friends before either of them was born. Michael couldn't remember a time when Zack wasn't in his life.

In the picture, they were wearing their Little League uniforms. Each one was holding a bat against his shoulder. Zack's bat had his mitt hanging off the end of it.

Michael went to see it up close. All the little details appeared to be right. Zack looked like Zack. Their uniforms were the right colors: white with blue. The team name was also right— **WILDCATS** in bold letters across the front.

Then he went to his computer. The screensaver was showing all sorts of other pictures. Michael sat there for a moment and watched them. Those of him and Zack were right. So were those of his mom and dad. But the two of Corinne were both wrong. They showed the girl he just saw in the living room. In one, they were at a restaurant for his birthday. There was a cake in front of him, and the girl was hugging him from behind. The other picture showed them at the beach. He was buried up to his waist in the sand. And she was pouring more sand onto him from a red plastic bucket.

He got up and went to the closet. He opened the door slowly, then turned on the light. There were shirts on hangers, pants on the shelves, and shoes and sneakers on the floor. He checked out the shoes and sneakers first.

Those black dress shoes are right, he thought. His mom bought them to go along with his one suit. He hated the shoes to death. And he hated the suit even more. *But at least they're both right*, he told himself. Then there was his collection of Converse shoes. He had a bunch of different colors. But some of them were wrong. The navy blues were still there. And he still didn't remember receiving them as a gift, as his dad had suggested. Another pair was bright red, like a fire truck. A third pair was as purple as a plum. The pair next to that was canary yellow.

"I would never have purple sneakers," he mumbled to himself. "Or red, or yellow. I *hate* the color yellow."

He sat on the bed and rubbed the sides of his head. Then he took his phone off the nightstand. He couldn't decide if he wanted to tell Zack what had been happening. He didn't want his best friend to think he was going crazy. But now he didn't care anymore. Talking to Zack about stuff always made him feel better.

He unlocked his phone. Then he started a new text. But Zack's name didn't come up in the phone's memory.

Huh?!

He'd been having trouble with the phone

since the last OS update. Some of the other apps stopped working. And a few of his photos had disappeared.

"Don't tell me all the contacts were wiped out, too," he said angrily.

Michael turned the phone around. He always kept a small piece of paper between the phone and its case. The case was clear, so the paper was easy to see. It had a few phone numbers written on it—Dad, Mom, Corinne, Zack, and some others. He kept the list in case the memory ever got wiped out.

"Okay," he said, "Zack is two-three-two, eight-four-sev—"

His mouth snapped shut when he saw the phone's logo. It wasn't an apple—it was a pear. It still had the bite taken out of it on the right side. It also had a little leaf attached to the stem at the top. The leaf was pointing to the left.

He stared at the pear. His brain felt like it was beginning to overload.

No, it's supposed to be an apple…I'm sure of it. The Apple company, started by Steve Jobs. They make iPhones and iPads and iPods and all that stuff…

Don't they?

He got the sense that reality was slipping away from him. Slipping through his fingers like jelly.

"You're okay," he said through heavy breaths. "It's fine. It's all good. There's an explanation for this." He started nodding. "Yeah, there's an explanation, and you're going to figure it out. You and Zack. He'll help you figure it out. He's your best friend."

He looked back at the list of phone numbers. Zack's was the fourth one down.

"Okay…two-three-two, eight-four-seven-si—" He stopped again. Only this time his mouth didn't snap shut. It just hung there like it was on broken hinges. His eyes opened wide, then even wider. They were locked on the name next to the number. It was in his own handwriting. But it didn't say "Zack"—it said "Dylan."

He didn't have a friend named Dylan.

He didn't even *know* anyone named Dylan.

He began screaming.

Loudly.

Dr. Bergman was a very nice man. He was thin and tall, with white hair that was just about gone on top. His hands shook sometimes, which Michael didn't like at all. But he had been the Cooper family's doctor since forever. And the fact that he lived just two doors down from them was nice.

He sat on the bed next to Michael and shined a light in his eyes. Then he put the palm of his hand on Michael's forehead. After that he stuck one finger in the air. It looked like he was pointing at the ceiling.

"Okay, Mike, keep an eye on this."

He moved the finger from left to right.

Then right to left. Michael followed it with no problem. It looked like he was watching a tennis match.

"Well?" his mom asked. She was standing just behind Dr. Bergman. And his dad was standing next to her.

The doctor shook his head. "I don't see any sign of…y'know, major problems."

Fear rolled across Michael's face like a cloud. "Problems? You mean like brain damage? How can I—"

"Shh…take it easy," Dr. Bergman said, patting his hand. "I'm not saying anything like that. But I have to start with the big stuff and work down from there."

"Oh…okay, sure."

"You've obviously been quite sick."

"Yeah, I have."

"And I understand you've been

hallucinating."

"Doesn't that mean, like, seeing things?" Michael asked.

"Yes."

"Well…no, I haven't been hallucinating."

One of Dr. Bergman's eyebrows went up. "Oh? That's not what your mom and dad told me."

"It means seeing things that aren't really there, right?"

"That's correct."

"The things I've been seeing really *are* there!"

"Like the bathroom door changing from one side of the hall to the other?" the doctor asked.

Michael didn't like the way he said this. He sounded like he thought Michael was a complete idiot.

"That's what I saw! And no one's going to tell me different!"

"Michael!" his mom said sharply. "Do *not* talk to Dr. B that way!"

Dr. Bergman waved his hand in the air. "No, it's okay. I can imagine how he feels." Then, back to Michael, he said, "You don't need to get upset, Michael. Just understand that things like that are impossible, okay? Doors really don't move around. Purple sneakers don't just show up in someone's closet. And your sister is still your sister. Got it?"

Michael lay there with his arms folded, saying nothing. *They all think I've lost it,* he thought. *They're not saying so, but they do.*

"You just need some rest," Dr. Bergman said. Then he took a bottle of pills out of his pocket. "These aren't very strong. We'll give you just one, and it'll help you fall asleep."

"I don't *want* to sleep!" Michael replied. "Every time I wake up, more things change!"

The doctor smiled. "Not this time, Michael. This time will be different, you'll see."

"Go ahead, Michael," his mom said. "It'll be okay."

"Yeah," his dad added. "You'll be fine, kiddo."

A tiny pill was put in Michael's hand. Then his mom got him a glass of water from the bathroom. (*I wonder what side of the hall the door is on this time*, he couldn't help thinking.) He put the pill in his mouth. Then he drank the water to wash it down.

He lay back on the pillow. His eyelids began to feel heavy. It was hard keeping them open. He heard Dr. Bergman saying, "This time will be different" over and over in his mind. The voice was all echoey.

Then, just before he fell asleep, he heard his own voice say something back—

I hope you're right…

I hope you're right…

I hope you're right…

Michael slept for a long time. And when he finally opened his eyes, he *felt* like he'd been asleep for a long time.

He lay there staring at the ceiling. Then the terrible, bone-gripping fear immediately began flooding back into him. He remembered everything. The bathroom door being in the wrong place…

His sister *not* being his sister…

Zack being renamed Dylan…

It all thundered into his brain in a rush of terrifying images.

He saw that the ceiling was a light yellow. His heart, which had been pounding away, slowed just a little. That much seemed right to him, and he let himself feel a little better. Maybe Dr. Bergman had been telling the truth. Maybe it was going to be okay. *I just needed some rest*, he told himself. *But it's all going to be fine now. All back to normal.* This is what he believed for a few seconds.

A few seconds after that, he realized how wrong he was.

"Wait a second," he said. "No…the ceiling *isn't* supposed to be yellow."

His eyes went next to the closet door. He wondered if it had changed places like the one in the hallway. And it had—it was a few feet from where it was supposed to be.

"Oh no…" This came out as a whisper because he had almost no breath in his lungs.

He sat up and looked around the rest of the room. So many things were different.

The dresser was on the other side. And the picture he took with Zack was on top of it. It had been on the wall before he fell asleep. There was also a third kid in it. They all had their arms around each other. Michael had no idea who the other kid was.

He threw the sheets back and got out of bed. He expected to feel the cool carpet under his bare feet. But there was no carpet anymore. It was bare wood. Then he saw that his poster of the New York Yankees was gone. In its place was a poster for the Washington Nationals. Michael had never watched a Nationals game in his life. He didn't know their record this season. He didn't know the names of any players. Or even their coach.

His brain was overloading again. Another memory came to him. When he and Zack were little, their moms would take them to Curtis Park. It had lots of swings and a big jungle gym. But Michael's favorite thing was the merry-go-round. He loved to get it spinning really fast. Then he'd lie on his back and let his head hang over the edge while it zoomed around. A weird feeling always came over him. It was like he was about to lose control and go flying.

That's how he felt now—like his mind was right at the edge, about to go flying…

Then he saw a small model airplane on his dresser.

"No," he said. "That's supposed to be a car. A 2018 Camaro ZL1 convertible! Not a *plane*!"

With shaking hands, he opened the dresser's top drawer. T-shirts were folded neatly inside. And that's where he always kept them.

But none of them were right.

He took one out. It was red with a big surfer graphic—and he had never seen it before. He'd never even surfed before, or even *thought* about surfing. Another had a cartoon gecko in a pair of sunglasses. Michael liked the gecko just fine. But not so much that he wanted him on a T-shirt.

He felt his stomach roll over.

No…don't throw up…please don't throw up…

But he thought he might. Everything had started moving around down there.

"The garbage can," he said. But when he turned, he saw that it wasn't next to the TV anymore.

Don't throw up…oh please, don't throw up…

He went to the closet and grabbed the doorknob. Then he stopped. Only a small part of him really wanted to know what was inside.

But that small part of him was also stronger than all the others. He had to see. He didn't want to—but he *had* to.

With his heart pounding, he opened the door.

At first, everything seemed okay. Shirts on hangers. Pants on the shelves up top. Shoes and sneakers on the floor.

Then he looked closer. Just like the T-shirts, these were all different. Some of the pants were khakis and some were cotton slacks. Before, they were almost all jeans.

And the hanging shirts used to be plain colors. Either white or light blue. Now there were bright pinks and greens and yellows. A few even had stripes.

"No…these aren't mine."

The Converse collection was gone. It had been replaced by Adidas and Nikes.

The black dress shoes were still there—along with two other pairs. One was brown, the other tan.

Michael pulled a shirt off its hanger. It was light pink, with long sleeves and buttons down the front. When it came to clothes, he hated pink above all other colors. He also didn't like button-down shirts in general. He wore them only when he had to, like at a family party or whatever. But even then, he would never put on a pink one.

He went to throw the shirt on the bed. Then he saw the tag inside, and his heart skipped a beat.

The word **SMALL** was printed in tiny capital letters.

"I'm a *medium*," he said sharply. "I haven't been a small since fourth gr—"

Then all the color drained out of his face.

He turned back to the closet and began checking the tags on the other shirts. They were all smalls.

He went to the pants next. The first pair he grabbed were khakis. He unfolded them to see the tag on the inside seam. "12S" was printed above the washing instructions.

"No...I'm a *fourteen* S. Fourtee—"

He stood there breathing hard for a few seconds, his eyes shifting all over.

Then he said, "Wait...Oh no...no, no, no, no, no....*NO WAY*!!!"

He dropped the pants and ran for the door. Pulling it back, he saw that everything in the hallway was different, too.

The pale-green carpet was light blue. And the wallpaper didn't have the floral pattern anymore. Now it was all sorts of floating shapes, like circles and triangles.

The door to the bathroom was on the right side again. Michael didn't open it right away. Instead, he turned around slowly.

There were four framed pictures on the wall now. All were family photos. In one, everybody was at what looked like an outdoor wedding. In another, they were going down the log flume at some theme park. In the third, they were all flying kites in a big open field.

The fourth was a posed photo in a studio somewhere. Everyone was wearing the same thing—blue jeans and plain, white T-shirts. They all looked happy. And you could tell they all got along and really loved each other.

The kind of family anyone would want to be a part of. There was just one problem—

Michael didn't recognize any of them.

He began to tremble all over. It was as if a cold breeze had suddenly blown over him. Then his mouth tried to shape certain words, but no sounds came out.

He turned back to the bathroom door. He opened it and stepped inside. Then he saw that the toilet, sink, and shower had been shuffled around. And the colors weren't the same. Neither were the lights.

But that wasn't the scariest thing at the moment...

He closed his eyes and stepped in front of the sink. He swallowed into a throat that was as dry as an old chimney. His breathing was so hard that he could hear it clearly.

Please...please no...please oh please oh please...

He opened his eyes. He looked in the mirror. And he saw exactly what he feared.

Like the people in the hallway photos, the person staring back at him was a complete stranger.

Michael ran out of the bathroom screaming his head off. He didn't go back to his room, but toward the kitchen.

When he got there, however, he saw that it wasn't the kitchen anymore. It was the living room. His dad's easy chair was gone. So was the little table that had always stood next to it. There were two big couches instead of one. The light-brown carpet had become a light-gold carpet. And the front door to the house was on the left side of the big window rather than the right.

"Danny, what are you screaming about?" someone asked from upstairs.

Michael froze. *Who is THAT? And who's Dann—no, don't tell me...you've got to be kidding...*

A man came thumping down the steps. He had broad shoulders and light hair. Reading glasses were perched on the end of his nose. And he was carrying papers in one hand and a pen in the other.

"I'm trying to pay some bills, sporto," he said. "Can you keep it down a little?"

Michael had never seen this person in his life.

"I...I'm sorry. I'll try to be—wait, *who are you?*"

The man smiled and sniffed a little laugh through his nose.

"Good one, Danny. It's nice to know we have a comedian in the family."

"I'm serious," Michael said, trying to

sound tough but falling way short. "I don't know who you are. Or why you're in my house."

One of the man's eyebrows went up. "Dan," he said flatly. "I really do have to pay these bills. If I don't, we won't have any water, gas, or electricity. So unless you're trying to—"

"Phillip, what's going on?" asked a new voice.

Michael spun around and found another stranger standing there. She had just walked in the room. She was short, with strawberry-blond hair that fell straight down the sides of her face.

"I'm not sure, Kate," the man on the steps replied. "Either our son here is having a complete mental breakdown. Or, more likely, he's in one of his goofy moods again."

The woman walked over until she was about two feet away. She looked at Michael curiously.

"Are you feeling all right, Danny?"

"My name isn't Danny," he said, his eyes wild with fear. "It *isn't*."

The man shook his head. "I don't know what's wrong with him," he said. Then he turned and headed back upstairs. "But if you figure it out, let me know."

The woman stepped closer. Then she reached up toward Michael's face.

He jerked back. "What are you doing?"

"I just want to feel your forehead."

Michael didn't want her to do it, but he let her. She did it gently, just like a mother would. And her hand was warm, solid. A *real* hand.

So if this is a dream, he thought, *it's the most detailed dream I've ever had.*

"You feel a little warm," she said. "How's

your stomach?"

"My stomach's fine," he replied. This wasn't even close to the truth. His stomach felt like it was being squeezed by a giant hand.

But he wasn't about to tell this person anything.

"I'm making roast chicken," she said. "Do you want some? Maybe you need to eat."

"No, I'm not hungry." This was also a lie, as he was basically starving. He hadn't really eaten since this whole weird thing started. But the last thing he wanted right now was food.

"Then maybe you should—"

"Hey, Mom!" another unknown voice called out. It also came from upstairs.

"I'm here, sweetie!" the woman yelled back. Then came the sound of footsteps pounding down the steps.

Michael turned, his face turning pale. The person who appeared a moment later wasn't his sister. In fact, it wasn't a girl at all.

The boy was maybe a year or two older. He was tall and thin, with curly brown hair that hung beyond his ears. He was wearing Vans that were nearly falling apart. His jeans had ragged holes in the knees. And his T-shirt said:

I RIDE A SKATEBOARD BECAUSE RUNNING STINKS.

He saw Michael and smiled. "Hey, Dan the Man! What's up, little bro?" When Michael didn't answer, the boy turned to the woman and said, "What's wrong with him?"

"I don't know," she replied. She put her hands on her hips and said, "Danny, maybe I should bring you to the doc—"

"*Stop*!" Michael said, holding his hands up. "Just stop it, all of you! Who *are* you? Where did you come from? *AND WHERE DID MY FAMILY GO?*"

"Dude, chill out," the boy said. "What are you, crazy?"

"Danny, come on, let's get you to see Dr. Clarke." She put a hand under his elbow, but he pulled it away.

"I don't know any Dr. Clarke! My doctor is Dr. Bergman! And you're not my family!"

"Danny…" the woman said.

"AND MY NAME'S NOT DANNY!!!" he shot back. "*IT'S…IT'S…*"

He wanted to scream out *MICHAEL*!!!

Then he decided there was no point in doing that.

He turned and ran as fast as he could.

Michael found the kitchen because he knew that's where the door would be. It was in a different place—of course it was—but at least it was *there*.

He yanked it open and went outside. There was a driveway that ran alongside the house. That much, at least, was the same. But the cars parked in it were all different. His dad drove a black Ford truck, and his mom had a white Volkswagon Beetle convertible. Neither of those cars was anywhere in sight. Instead, there was a green Honda and a silver Mercedes coupe.

He went past them, reached the sidewalk,

and turned right.

As he ran, he saw that many things on the street had changed. Mrs. Simmons, who lived next door, loved to garden. And she had lots of colorful flowers in her front yard. But they were all gone now. There were a few bushes in their place, but they were overgrown and scraggly.

Mr. Carter's house was painted light red. It was supposed to be white.

The Kontoleons had a holly tree on the right side of their front walk. It should have been on the left.

The mailbox on the corner of Spruce and Maple was missing.

So was the fire hydrant that usually sat next to it.

And the roads weren't named Spruce and Maple anymore. Now they were Lincoln and

Washington.

Michael got to the corner and turned left this time. He had started crying, although he was hardly aware of it. Every inch of his body ached. From being scared, from being stressed, from being tired and hungry. But he kept on running. He wasn't even sure where he wanted to go.

He reached the intersection of what used to be Maple and Sycamore. Now it was Lincoln and Roosevelt. When all cars had passed, he crossed over. Then he ran again until he came to the park. He didn't expect it to still be named Curtis—and it wasn't. The wooden sign now said Gulliver Park. And underneath the name was the line:

MAINTAINED BY THE TOWN OF
Hillford

"No," Michael said, shaking his head as more tears came. "It's supposed to say Queenstown! *Queenstown*!"

This was the breaking point for him. He simply could not take any more. He stood there with his arms at his sides, crying like a baby.

"What is going *ON*?" he moaned. The last word came out more like a screech.

He forced himself to walk across the grass and past the jungle gym. There was a bench on the other side. This is where parents would sit and watch their kids.

He dropped onto it. Then he buried his face in his hands and cried even more. He had absolutely no idea what to do. He didn't know how any of this happened. So he couldn't even begin to guess how to fix it. He felt like a cork on the ocean, lost and drifting.

What…in the world…do I DO?

He thought hard, but no answers came. Then he felt the first pangs of something else. It was a sense of giving up. Of not caring anymore. Not about this, not about himself—not about *anything*.

He had never been the type of kid to give up. When he struggled in math class, he just worked harder at it. When he started in Little League, he found that he couldn't hit too well. So he practiced and practiced until he could.

He didn't believe in quitting. He believed in always pushing ahead.

Except for now, he told himself.

"I had a feeling you'd be like this," someone said.

Michael almost jumped out of his skin.

And when he looked, he found someone sitting on the other side of the bench.

He couldn't believe who it was.

Zack didn't look any different than usual. No different than he was *supposed* to. Same light brown hair, pointy chin, and wide smile. He was wearing a navy T-shirt with a big Yankees logo on it. He always wore that shirt, along with faded denim shorts. And he had those on, too. There was a Band-Aid on his left wrist. It covered a burn he got a few days ago from the toaster oven in his kitchen.

Michael was there when it happened. In fact, Michael had warned him to wear an oven mitt. But like always, Zack just had to take a chance. He reached in to get his chicken patty. Then his wrist touched the inside rim of the oven.

He yelped and dropped the patty on the floor. Michael called him an idiot. Zack told him to shut his face while he ran the burn under cold water. Then he put on a Band-Aid—the same one he had now.

It took Michael a moment to find his breath.

"What…what are you *doing* here?!"

"Nice way to talk to your best friend," Zack said with a chuckle. "Do you want me to go?"

"No! I just…I don't understand why… how…why are you here? And *how* are you here?"

"Because your parents told me what was happening. You're having a little trouble, it seems."

Michael looked more confused than ever. "You *know* about this?"

"You mean about the changes?"

"Yeah…"

"Of course. Everyone does."

"*WHAT*???"

"You mean your parents never told you?"

He looked at Zack like he was insane. "What are you talking about?!"

Zack laughed again and shook his head. "Don't feel too bad, Mikey. My parents didn't tell me until I was twelve. But I didn't realize your parents never told you at *all*!"

"Zack, what in the world—"

"The *changes*, dude! The ones that happen every couple of years."

Michael got that feeling again. Like being on the edge of a merry-go-round, just about to fly off.

"I have no idea what that means," he said.

Zack rubbed his hands together, then held them apart. "Okay, I'll tell it to you the way my parents told me."

"Uh-huh…"

"Every few years, people go through these changes."

"What people? Who?"

"Everybody."

"*Everybody*?!"

"Yeah. Everything in their life just kind of *changes*. Their family, their friends, their house, whatever. It's a transformation. Like…remember in health class when we learned about our bodies? How they become completely new about once every seven or eight years?"

Michael did remember this, because he found it fascinating. When cells in the human body became worn out, new ones were produced. After about seven years, every old cell had been replaced by a new one.

"Yeah," Michael said. "I remember."

"It's sort of like that. Just like our bodies

change, so does everything else around us. And that includes our memories. They change with everything else. That way, we don't *realize* the changes have happened. Our memories kind of get updated."

Michael thought about this for a moment. He was always willing to hear new ideas and learn new things. But this sounded ridiculous.

"Uh…no," he said, "that can't be true. I remember *everything* that's different now. I remember the way it all was before."

Zack laughed out loud and nodded. "That's the problem—something went wrong with you this time."

"*This* time?"

"Yeah. Everything went smoothly all the other times. It happens about every two or three years on average. I mean, come on. Is it really so bad? Getting a kind of 'family upgrade' every now and then?"

"Zack, you've lost your cookies if you think I'm going to believe any of this. And I remember lots of things from the last two or three years. Heck, I remember things from *ten* years ago!"

"Oh? Like what?"

Michael scanned his mind for anything that really stood out.

"Like…okay, remember the time you got stung by that bee? You were in my pool and you reached for that toy boat. There was a bee on top of it, and you didn't see it. You got stung, and you—what's wrong?"

Zack was smiling patiently, like a parent would.

"Mikey, you don't have a pool."

"Uh, yes I do."

"Prove it."

"All right, let me see your phone."

Zack pulled it out of his pocket and handed it over. "There you go," he said cheerfully.

Michael opened the photo collection and scrolled through it with his finger. Zack had thousands, so Michael sorted them by date. *Last August…last August…*

"A-ha!" he said, then tapped on one file in particular. "Right here is—"

The image did show Michael in his backyard with Zack. But they weren't in the pool. And that's because there wasn't one. In its place was a big yard of nice, thick grass. They were throwing a Frisbee back and forth.

"You *deleted* the photo with the pool!" Michael said angrily.

"I did no such thing."

"Then you changed it somehow. In Photoshop or something."

Zack rolled his eyes. "Come on, Mike. I

don't even *have* Photoshop. And even if I did, I don't know the first thing about it. Look again. Look *closely*. That photo's as real as any other."

Michael put two fingers on the screen and spread them apart. The photo became too big to see all at once. But that was what he wanted. He needed to see all the little details. And once he did…

It does look real, he admitted to himself. *No— it IS real. Not faked at all.*

"Okay," he said, "then what about the time we went to King's Pizza? Remember, you spilled soda all over yourself? And you made me take a picture with your phone? Because you wanted to post it on AllMyFriends.com?"

"Go ahead and look for it," Zack said.

"I will."

Michael scrolled through the pictures again. He found the right date—September 6. This was easy to remember because it was the day before school started.

When he tapped on the file, however, something very different opened up. They were all at Golden Garden. It was the Chinese takeout place across the street from King's. They were sitting in a little booth waiting for their order.

"No…" Michael said. "This isn't right! This is not what happened!"

Zack took the phone back and replaced it in his pocket.

"That's because everything has been *changing*," he said. "Jeez, don't you get it?"

"No, I don't get it at all."

"Mikey, our memories change so we *don't* remember what it was like before."

"That's ridiculous."

"Is it?" Zack pointed to the Band-Aid on his arm. "What happened to me here?"

"You burned yourself on your toaster oven."

"No, I scraped it on one of my mom's rosebushes. See?"

He tore one side of the Band-Aid off. The wound didn't look like a burn at all. It looked like…

A scrape.

"I was there when it happened!" Michael yelled. "You *burned* yourself!"

Zack was shaking his head. "No, that's just what you think you remember."

"Okay, then how come I *know* everything's changing? If our memories are supposed to change, how come mine hasn't?"

Zack threw his hands up. "I have no idea. It happens sometimes. I've heard of it happening to other people. I guess you're just one of the unlucky ones. At least this time…" He paused a moment, then added, "Next time it'll probably be fine."

Every gear in Michael's brain was cranking at full speed. A part of him was starting to believe it all. How could he deny what Zack was showing him? Zack was his best friend—he wouldn't lie. His honesty was one of the things Michael liked best about him. He did stupid stuff sometimes. And he could be oh-so annoying. But he was always honest. There was no doubt about that.

"I never had any idea," Michael said softly.

"Well, you're not supposed to," Zack said. "That's the point of what I'm telling you."

"But what if I don't *want* things to change?"

"Ah, well—there's nothing you can do about it, Mikey. It's just a part of life."

Michael shook his head. He loved his family so much. He knew he didn't tell them that often enough. But now that he was faced with the idea of losing them…

A deep sadness poured into him. He didn't want them to disappear. He didn't care if his "new" family was nice or whatever. He wanted to be with the family he'd known all his life. (Or he *thought* he'd known all his life.) And live in the house he'd always lived in. With all the same rooms…and all of his clothes…and his Converse sneakers…

There has to be a way to stop the change, he told himself. *There has to be.*

"Okay, tell me this. *Why* do these changes happen?"

Zack smiled. It was the weirdest smile Michael ever saw. It was as if it didn't fit Zack somehow. Like it was someone *else's* smile, but on Zack's face.

"I think you know the answer to that question," he replied. Zack's voice was strange, too. It wasn't his at all. It belonged to someone older, someone wiser. But Michael didn't know who.

He looked away from Zack then. And when he did, he realized that all the things around them had been changing while they were talking. And not just changing, but *fading*. It was like in a movie, where the screen grows darker until it's all black.

In that moment, Michael understood everything.

He turned back and said, "I know! It's because I didn't appreciate what I—"

Then he stopped, because Zack was gone.

A bolt of fear shot through Michael's body. He looked all around, but there was no sign of his best friend anywhere. It was like Zack had never been there in the first place. He was completely alone.

Even worse, everything else in the park continued to fade away. The trees, the jungle gym, the swings…everything. They faded at different speeds, too. At first he could kind of see through them. Then they vanished altogether. After the jungle gym disappeared, only the bed of wood chips on the ground remained. Then that also started fading. The trees were also going one by one, in what seemed like random order.

But the most frightening part of it all was the darkness. When certain things disappeared, there was nothing behind them. Just a black shape where those things had been. It was like taking a piece out of a jigsaw puzzle that was lying on black paper or something. And Michael realized it wasn't really some kind of weird black surface he was seeing. It was *nothingness*. It was the total lack of anything. Pure emptiness. A world with holes in it. A world that was disappearing forever.

"No!" he cried as he jumped from the bench. "*NO!!!*"

He started running forward, but things kept vanishing. First a little water fountain, then a sign saying the park closed after dark.

He turned back and watched in horror as the bench went from being there to not being there.

"No!" he yelled again, not even sure who might be listening. "I understand now! Please don't do this!" Tears rolled down his cheeks in shiny streams. "*I UNDERSTAND NOW AND I'M SORRY!!!*"

But it didn't help. Everything just kept fading. The fence around the tennis courts… the tennis courts themselves…the row of houses behind them…

Finally, Michael was surrounded by nothing but darkness. And then he felt himself begin to fade, too. The darkness didn't just surround him now. It came *into* him. He could feel his thoughts begin to float away. He started losing his awareness of everything. Reality—or what was left of it—began to spin. Slowly at first, then faster. He could still hear himself crying, but it didn't matter anymore. He went down, like water into a drain.

Then it was over.

Michael's eyes fluttered open. The first thought that came to him was, *I feel like I've been asleep forever*. He saw nothing but white. Pure white in every direction.

Then he realized he was looking at his bedroom ceiling.

"Just…just like it's supposed to be!" he said out loud.

He lifted his head off the pillow and looked around. Then came a wave of relief, followed by incredible happiness.

Everything in the room was back to normal.

The dresser was on the left side again. The

little garbage can was next to the TV. The framed photo of him and Zack was hanging on the wall. And there was no third kid in the picture. It was *just* him and Zack.

He threw the sheets back and got out of bed. His feet touched the carpet, and that made him even happier.

He went to the closet and opened the door. On the top shelf, there was nothing but jeans.

Yes.

On the hangers, there were very few button-down shirts. And none that were pink.

Yes!

On the floor was a bunch of Converse sneakers—in all the colors that he loved.

YES!!!

He went to the dresser next. The model airplane was gone, and the 2018 Camaro ZL1 convertible was back. Its shiny silver body gleamed in the morning sunlight.

Dreams, he thought then. *They were all dreams. Very detailed, but still…just very bad dreams.*

He took the car in hand and lay back down on the bed. Then the door opened, and someone leaned in.

Michael smiled. "Dad!"

It was him all right. Tall and thin, with those same silver streaks in his hair.

"I thought I heard you moving around in here," he said quietly. Then, turning back to the hallway, he called, "Hon? He's awake!" A moment later they were both in the room. And he saw that his mom had also returned to normal.

"So how are you feeling?" his dad asked. He stood at the foot of the bed with his hands in his pockets.

Michael shrugged. "Okay, I guess. But you won't believe the weird dreams I've been having."

"Oh, I think I would."

Michael looked at him, confused. "What do you mean?"

"How's your head?" his mom asked before his dad had a chance to answer.

"Strange. Like my brain is floating around loose in my skull or something."

"Mild dizziness?"

"Yeah."

She nodded. "Dr. Bergman said that might happen after…well, afterward."

"Afterward? After *what*?" When neither of them replied, he said, "What's going on?"

His parents looked to each other for a moment. They were acting strange. And it took Michael a moment to find just the right word in his head. *Embarrassed*, he decided finally. *That's it—they seem very embarrassed.*

"Uh, Michael," his dad began. "Do you

remember when you were sick about a week ago?"

Michael thought back. So many bizarre things had been happening lately. It wasn't easy separating the facts from the fiction.

Then it came to him.

"I had a bad cold, right?"

His dad nodded. "You did. Really bad. You were blowing your nose every two minutes. And running a high fever, too."

"That's right, I remember. So?"

"Okay, well…" His dad shuffled his feet and looked down at the carpet.

"Come on, Dad! What's the big secret?"

His mom finally said, "Your dad and I have been giving you the wrong medicine."

Michael stared at them for a long moment. He was waiting for some sign that they were joking. When none came, he said, "You're kidding."

"No," his mom replied. "We're not."

"*That's* what's been happening to me?"

His dad nodded. "I'm afraid so. They gave us the wrong medicine at the drug store. But still…we should have checked first. You should always check once, twice, three times when it comes to medication."

Michael laughed. "Okay, it all makes sense now. But wow…that was *crazy*!"

"Dr. Bergman told us you might, um… start seeing things a little bit," his mom said.

"More than a *little* bit!" Michael said. Then he told them about every terrifying vision he'd had over the last few days.

"Yeah…" his dad said, nodding. "That sounds about right. That medicine makes your imagination go crazy. Just like Dr. Bergman said it would."

His mom sat down on the bed. "Michael, we're so sorry," she said. "Can you please forgive us?"

He leaned forward and hugged her.

"Only if you'll forgive me, too."

"For what?"

"For being so mean to you guys while I was sick. You, Corinne, everybody."

His dad reached over and patted him on the back.

"It's okay, kiddo. We understand."

"Maybe," Michael said, "but it's still not okay. You guys were only trying to take care of me. I know that. I should've been nicer. But you guys are the best. I have the best family in the world. The best family, the best friends, the best *life*. I'm never going to forget that ever again. Because you have to appreciate the people and things that you care about. If you don't, they'll…

well, they'll go away."

His dad laughed. "Wow, how sick *were* you?"

Michael thought carefully before answering.

"Sick enough," he said. "But I'm better now."

And I'm going to stay that way, he told himself.

Want to Keep Reading?

Turn the page for a sneak peek at
the next book in the series.

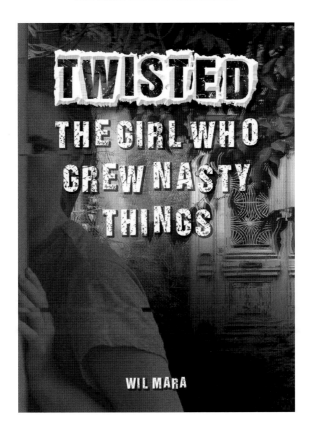

ISBN: 9781538383667

Maddie Dragonette sat by herself in a quiet corner of the school cafeteria. She sat at this same table every day. It was a small table with just one chair. It was used sometimes by the cafeteria's workers. Someone might sit and wrap sets of silverware into fresh napkins. Or write out the menu that would go on the school bulletin board. But during lunch period, the table was left open for Maddie. This wasn't an official rule or anything. It was just kind of understood.

Maddie sat by herself because she wanted to. She couldn't stand her classmates. For that matter, she really couldn't stand *anyone*. Other people made her angry. In fact, whenever she thought about them, she didn't even use the word "other." She just used the word "people," like she wasn't a person herself. And that's because, deep down, she *didn't* think of herself as a person. She wasn't sure what she was, exactly. But she was absolutely certain that she wasn't one of *them*. She was better.

People made her angry. She didn't like the way they walked. She didn't like the way they talked. She didn't like their clothes, their shoes, or their hair. She didn't like that some girls played on the school's softball team. She hated softball. And because she hated it, she thought everyone else should hate it, too. And anyone who didn't hate it—well, she hated them for *not* hating it.

She hated social studies, too. So she hated everyone who liked it. One of the boys in her social studies class was named Jordan. He was the smartest kid in the school. Maddie *really* hated that. She hated all the kids who were smart. And that's because, deep down, she knew she really wasn't too bright. She would never be as smart as Jordan. Or Billy Palmer. Or Allie Moskowitz. Or any of the smart kids. So she hated them, and that took care of that.

She had decided long ago that hating people was the answer to all of her problems.

Maddie unpacked her lunch from the brown paper bag. Then she unwrapped her sandwich and took a bite. It was chicken with lettuce, tomato, and mayo. As she chewed, she looked at the sandwich carefully. Her mother had made it that morning. The chicken looked good. All white meat, shredded into little pieces. There was the right amount of mayo. And the lettuce was nice and crisp.

But the tomato…that was a problem.

There was a spot in the middle where it was orange instead of red. And it was hard, too. Maddie didn't like that one bit. She liked having the best of everything. She felt she deserved it. And this wasn't the best sandwich it could have been. So she made a note in her mind. She was going to talk to her mother about the tomato when she got home. She might even do more than talk. She might have to yell a little. That was okay, though. Yelling at people was one thing Maddie Dragonette did love. It made her feel great.

She took another bite and looked around the cafeteria. It was really crowded at the moment. Some of the other kids were classmates of hers. They paid no attention to her. They never did. It was like she wasn't even there. They all talked and laughed and had a good time.

Something about this really bothered her. Seeing people happy…it just *bothered* her.

She made a point of looking at Olivia Robinson. Olivia was sitting with three other friends. They looked like they were having the greatest day ever. Maddie knew all about Olivia. She was a straight A student. She played field hockey, basketball, and—so gross—softball. She was a cheerleader. She had beautiful golden hair. She never said a bad word about anyone. And she was always cheerful. Sometimes Olivia sat and talked to people who *weren't* feeling cheerful. She was the type of person who really cared about others. Everyone loved her, and Maddie *really* hated that. She hated people who everyone else loved.

But none of that was important to Maddie right now. The important thing was what Olivia was holding. It was a beautiful necklace. It had a gold chain and a flower-shaped pendant. Maddie did like flowers. That's because she liked to grow things. Back home, she grew lots of things. Some were pretty. Some were not. A few were downright nasty. But that was okay. Nasty things could be useful sometimes.

Olivia held up the necklace so her friends could see it. Maddie had heard her talking about it in gym class. It was a gift from her aunt. Olivia had helped her clean out her basement last weekend. She also had the necklace's box, which had a little bow on top.

Maddie pretended she wasn't watching Olivia. But she was, very carefully. She was waiting, and she was getting tired of it. Olivia had her own sandwich out. She had put it on the table and unwrapped it. But she hadn't taken a bite yet. All she was doing was yapping about her precious necklace.

Olivia set it back in its box. Then she picked up the sandwich. She was about to take a bite. But she started laughing instead. One of her friends had said something funny. Maddie couldn't hear what it was, and she really didn't care.

Come on… she thought. *Come ON…*

Finally, Olivia took a bite. It was a big one. She chewed it around for a moment. It made her cheeks bulge, first on one side and then the other. Then she swallowed it. Maddie got a warm feeling in her own stomach. She had to fight back a smile.

Olivia started laughing again. Then everything changed. Her eyes grew wide, and her face began turning red. She started coughing. First only a little, then a lot. Her hands went to her throat. She tried to say something, but Maddie couldn't hear it. Now she looked really scared. All her friends did, too.

The one sitting next to her started rubbing her back. She asked Olivia what was wrong. Olivia said something about her sandwich being hot. Not *hot* hot, she said, but spicy hot.

ABOUT THE AUTHOR

Wil Mara has been an author for over 30 years and has more than 200 books to his credit. His work for children includes more than 150 educational titles for the school and library markets, and he has also ghostwritten five of the popular Boxcar Children mysteries. His 2013 thriller *Frame 232* reached the #1 spot in its category on Amazon and won the Lime Award for Excellence in Fiction. He is also an associate member of the NJASL, and an executive member of the Board of Directors for the New Jersey Center for the Book, an affiliate of the US Library of Congress. He lives with his family in New Jersey.

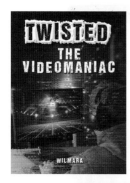
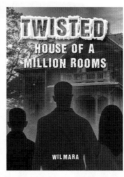

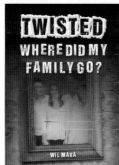